The Adventures of Santa Fe Sam

By Sandi Wright *Sandi Wright*
Illustrated by Riyon Harding

Santa Fe Sam is a Prairie Dog who lives in Santa Fe, New Mexico.

Sam lives in a hole underground. His home has a kitchen, a bedroom, a bathroom, and a living room.

Often, Burrowing Owls share these homes.

Sam lives with many other prairie dogs. Their burrows in the ground create a prairie dog town. Sam and his friends like running and playing above the burrows. From there, they can see cactus, sagebrush, tumbleweed, and tall mountains that are many miles away.

One day Sam sees an ant carrying a leaf larger than the ant herself! Sam follows the ant into prairie dog town and watches her go inside an ant hill where he notices something he has never seen before.

On the anthill, there is a pretty painting on a piece of clay. "What is this?" he wonders.

He sees a tall jackrabbit under a yucca plant nearby. "Mr. Jackrabbit, can you tell me what this is?" asks Sam.

The jackrabbit looked down where Sam placed the piece of clay at his feet and said, "Many, many years ago, a group of ancient peoples lived here.

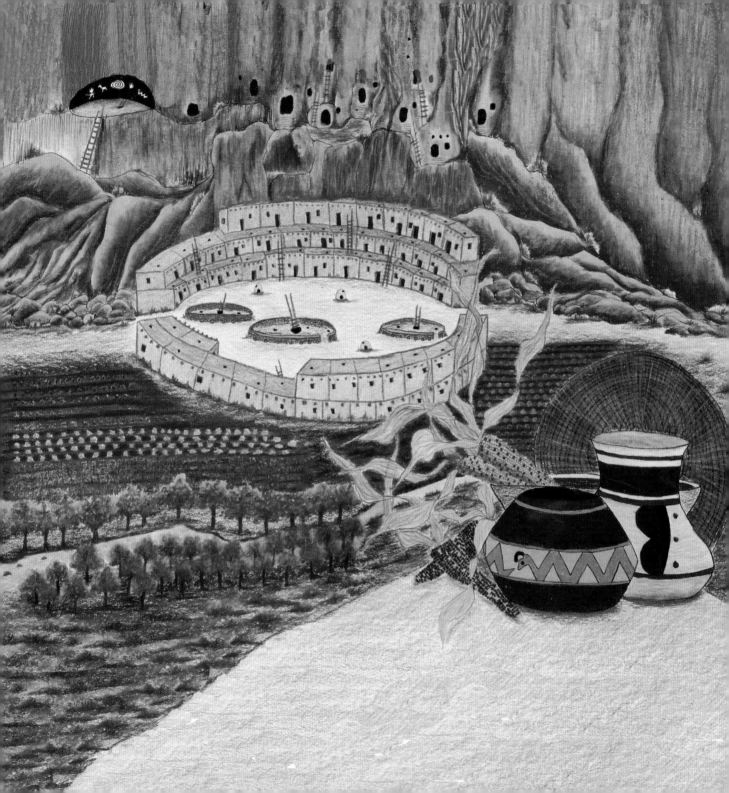

They lived in houses carved into the hills like caves. Later they built their homes made of bricks from the clay earth. These homes joined together like apartments, or even like your tunnels in prairie dog town, only above ground. We call them pueblos today. They made pots out of clay and placed them in the sun to dry. The ancient ones used the pots to store food, water, and for cooking," continued Jackrabbit.

"What you found is called a potshard."

"What is a potshard?" asks Sam.

"It is a chip from one of those ancient pots that was broken," answered Jackrabbit. "The pot makers chewed on the leaves of the yucca plant to make paintbrushes. They used them to paint and decorate the pots with clay colors and nature symbols. Your piece looks like a snake or lightening design."

"What happened to the ancient people?" Sam asked.

"No one knows for sure," Jackrabbit replied. "Many pueblo people living today trace their ancestry back to those ancient ones. In fact, this pottery piece may be an important link in the history of the pueblo people, so please leave it where you found it."

"Thank you," chirped Sam, and he hurried back to replace the treasure on the anthill.

A few days later Sam is out playing prairie dog games with his friends when the dark shadow of a hungry hawk passes over them. "Eck!" they yell and run every which way.

Sam dives into the nearest hole he can find. In there, he is safe.

On the bottom of the hole, Sam finds the prettiest rock he has ever seen. It is not a rock color; it is bright blue! He cannot believe his luck.

Lifting the pretty stone, he tries to take a bite. It is too hard to be food. It is not a potshard. He wants so badly to find out what it is and show the other prairie dogs but he has to wait until he knows the hawk is gone.

When Sam thinks it is safe,
he pokes his head out of the
hole, carefully looks around,
and makes a mad dash for
home with his new treasure.

Suddenly Sam trips over a giant rock. Only it is not a rock. It is Miss Tortoise taking a nap.

"Hello," Miss Tortoise says to a surprised Sam. "Where are you going in such a hurry?"

"I want to find someone who can tell me what this is," Sam says holding his pretty, blue rock to show Miss Tortoise.

"My, my, I have not seen a piece of turquoise this size in years," she says.

"What is turquoise?" Sam asks.

"It is a mineral found in the ground," she answers.

"What can you do with turquoise?" he asks.

"Come with me and I will show you," Miss Tortoise says.

At turtle speed, they walk to an old log. Pointing to a lovely piece of jewelry, Miss Tortoise says, "Look, the Native Americans have been using turquoise in their jewelry for many years. The Native Americans, once called Indians, are descendents of the early pueblo people."

Sam remembers what he just learned about the early pueblos and the ancient ones.

Miss Tortoise continued, "See how beautiful it is with the silver? You can visit downtown Santa Fe and see jewelry like this being sold on the plaza by the Native Americans."

Thanking Miss Tortoise, Sam returns home. He is happy and wants to tell his family and friends about his finds.

That night Sam is tucked in his bed fast asleep. Suddenly he is awakened by a large bolt of lightning striking a sage bush above his tunnel. "Kablam!" The thunder sounds like a train coming through his wall.

Sam is up in a flash and scampers outside to see what is happening. The bush is burning! He thumps his foot on the ground and barks out an alarm.

Immediately his dad is right beside him. "It's okay Sam," he says in a calm voice. "The fire is out now. Why don't you run down to the stream and get a bucket of water just in case."

Sam grabs his bucket and puts it into the stream. Just as he does, he notices something glittering in the moonlight. It is a shiny gold rock.

He forgets all about his bucket, he is so curious he has to know what it is.

Sam carries the rock to someone he thinks knows the answer. Mr. Owl lives in the tree just around the corner from the stream. He knows Mr. Owl is awake at this time of night.

"Mr. Owl, Mr. Owl," he calls, holding up his golden rock.

"Whooo goes?" replies the wise owl.

Sam answers, "It's only me, Sam. I found this in the stream! Do you have any idea what it is?"

"Why that's a gold nugget," the owl recalls. "Over one hundred years humans came here from all over the country to mine the gold. It was called the 'gold rush'.

Some gold was found in mines and streams in New Mexico but not enough, so the miners moved on to California to find their fortunes. Gold is worth a lot of money."

Sam thanks the owl and says good-bye. It is now daylight as he heads home. Along the way, he decides to pick some flowers for his mom beside where he dropped his bucket. Pulling up the first one, he sees a round metal object in the grass.

"Oh, I did not mean to scare you. What did you find in the flowers?" Ms. Butterfly asks.

"I hope you can tell me," Sam says, rubbing off the dirt and holding it closer to her. Ms. Butterfly knows what it is right away. She explains,

"That has been there for many years. A Spanish Conquistador dropped it there nearly five hundred years ago. He may have lost it while searching for gold for the King of Spain. It is a belt buckle. The Conquistadors did not find gold but instead found an enchanting new land full of ancient pueblos, buffalo, piñon nuts, pottery, turquoise, and prairie dogs just like you."

Ms. Butterfly continues, "These early explorers liked it here and stayed. The Hispanic people who live in New Mexico today are their descendants. Do you know that Santa Fe is the oldest capital city in the United States? Every year, the Santa Feans celebrate with a fiesta, or party, to which everyone is invited. They burn a huge puppet of ole man gloom to bring happiness to the town."

"Wow," thought Sam, the early Spanish settlers added a wonderful richness to his homeland in New Mexico." Sam even feels a little like a Conquistador himself, having found so many treasures. He leaves the buckle where he found it.

Sam thanks Ms. Butterfly for the history lesson and hurries home. His Mom greets him with a nose rub, which is the way prairie dogs kiss.

Inside his cozy home, Sam thinks about all the wonderful things he has learned. He feels tired but happy. His New Mexico land has shown him so many treasures.

His Santa Fe surroundings have such special stories to tell. Soon, he is asleep and dreaming of the fun adventures that lie ahead.

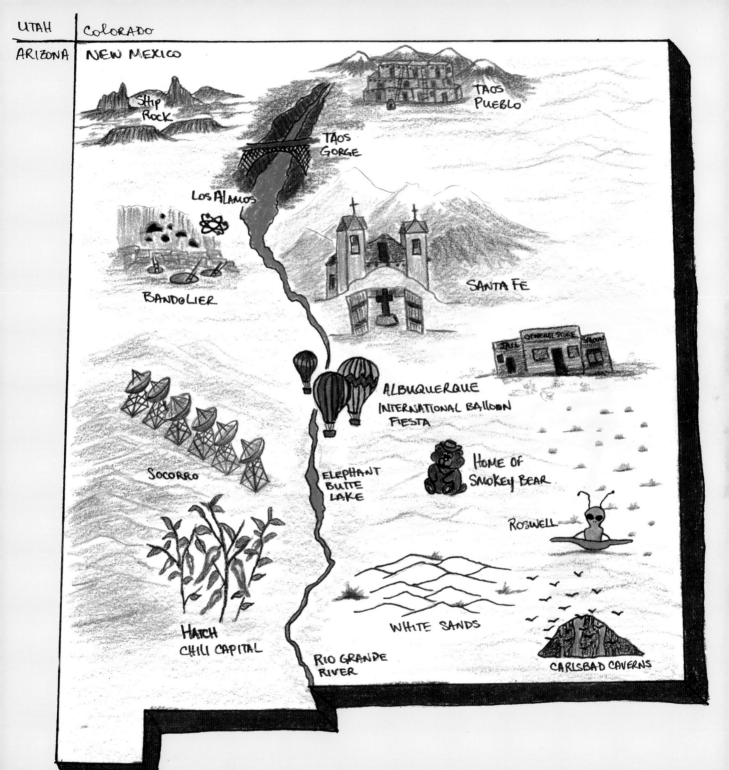

Acknowledgements

I have many people to thank for their valuable assistance and support throughout the production of this book. Without them, The Adventures Santa Fe Sam may have remained just a dream. First, I want to thank Sherry McGee (friend and beloved elementary school teacher of my daughters), who first turned me on to the idea of a creature who could tell the story of the history and the many cultures of Santa Fe that would be fit for children. This conversation was initiated by the arrival of her first grandchild, Emily. That was many years ago, but now, thanks to my daughter Shawndi, her husband Ted, and the birth of my own grandson, Owen, the idea was reinvigorated.

Second, I want to give a special thanks to Jared Gann, friend and fellow educator, without whose help in editing, computer skills, photographing and formatting along with a sunny disposition, "Sam" would never have made it off the mound.

Especially, I want to thank my other lovely daughter, Riyon, whose genius developed the prototype for "Sam." She captured the personalities of Santa Fe Sam and his friends in the beautifully illustrated drawings. Riyon made everything come to life in a delightful, enchanting way that only she could have done. I am blessed by all the talent and friendships that made this book possible.

Visit us online at http://santafesam.com.